MR. DUMP'S

CONSTIPATION CONSTERNATION

Roger Mee-Senseless

It was Monday morning and Mr Dump was running late as usual, when his phone rang.

RING, RING, RING, RING...

It was Mr Nice, who was calling from his nice phone in his nice new car.

"Morning Mr Dump, are you ready?" asked Mr Nice.

"Hold on, give me a few minutes," replied Mr Dump, "I just need to go and curl one out."

"Ok," said Mr Nice, "Just hurry up please."

25 minutes later Mr Dump emerged from his house and walked gingerly to Mr Nice's car, he carefully lowered himself into the seat.

"That was pretty savage." said Mr Dump. "I think I've given myself a hernia from pushing too hard, my arse is in bits. I don't get it, I'm normally like clockwork – 8 times a day at 2 hour intervals."

"Seriously, you don't need Big Ben or the talking clock when I'm around. Anyway, I've had to take a load of laxatives to try to loosen things up a bit."

"Have you ever heard of the phrase 'too much information'?" asked Mr Nice.

"Nope." replied Mr Dump.

Mr Dump spent the rest of the journey constantly changing the radio station.

He was searching for songs or lyrics
that could be vaguely poo related. He
shared these with Mr Nice. His
favourites were: Drop It Like It's
Hot, Free Fallin', Push It and Ring of
Fire.

Mr Nice spent the rest of the journey
thinking that he really needed to
find someone else to car share with.

He had been putting up with this
kind of thing for years and, despite
his niceness, had dark fantasies
involving Mr Dump and a 5,000 volt
cattle prod.

Mr Dump and Mr Nice worked at a plush office in the city centre. They were there to try to sell double glazing to the good people of Miandmrsland but, in reality, not many windows ever got sold by the ragtag bunch of employees including Mr Nice, Mr Quick, Little Miss Natterbox and Mr Dump.

Mr Nice's problem was that he was far too polite to sell anything despite being told numerous times per week by Mr Moody to fuck off.

I TELL YOU WHAT YOU CAN DO WITH YOUR WINDOWS - SHOVE THEM UP YOUR FAT, HAIRY ARSE - SIDEWAYS
shall I put you down as a maybe?

Mr Quick would get through lots of calls but he spoke so quickly that nobody could understand what he was saying. On the off chance that they did understand his machine gun delivery he would put the phone down on them if they hadn't agreed to buy within his self-imposed 45 second limit.

Little Miss Natterbox (who sat next to Mr Dump) would spend 95% of the day wittering on to her friends instead of actually making any sales calls.

yes hello I'm offering a special once in a lifetime deal not to be missed one day only buy one get one free windows they're proper top quality all the celebs have got these ones even Bob Carolgees. shall I book you in?
SUNGSAM

Mr Dump's problem was that he spent a similar amount of time on the toilet, today it was probably more like 98%.

One of the many problems of the business model at the company was that only 85 people lived in Mrandmrsland so they did tend to duplicate calls quite a lot. There is also a bit of a ceiling on how many times the same person will buy new windows every year. Even Mr Stupid, the companies best customer, cottoned on after his 5th set in six months.

The office was 'run' by Mr Dopey, who didn't have a clue what he was doing, let alone anyone else. If Mr Dump saw him in the corridor on his way to or from the toilet he would blag that he had to 'log out' and Mr Dopey would assume he was talking about the computer system.

At dinnertime Mr Dump plonked himself down next to Mr Nice in the canteen. Mr Nice was enjoying a nice home-made sheesh kebab.

"It's still all backed up." said Mr Dump.

"I've been on the toilet all morning and I feel like I'm gonna pop. I've had to take another handful of laxatives. I'm sure the turtle's head is out but it's not shifting."

Mr Nice pushed his sheesh kebab to one side.

"Are you going to Little Miss Sunbeam's birthday party later?" asked Mr Dump.

"Yeh, I might do." came the reply.

"Cool, can you pick me up at 8?" responded Mr Dump, in a flash.

"Actually, I've just remembered that I need to stay in and wash my hair." stammered Mr Nice.

"You don't have any hair?"

"FACE! I meant face!"

Later that evening Mr Dump arrived at Little Miss Sunbeam's home, after being forced to shell out for a taxi so that Mr Nice could spend the entire evening washing his mush.

"HAPPY BIRTHDAY!" said Mr Dump.

MR NICE 'WASHING HIS HAIR'

"Oh, hello Mr Dump. This is a surprise, I wasn't expecting you. Erm, did you get an invite?"

"I assumed it had been lost in the post," he said as he forced his way inside.

"I've got you a couple of presents." said Mr Dump.

"Oh, how very kind of you, I'll open them now."

She tore the wrapping paper from the first present which was a long, cylindrical shape.

"Wow, that's interesting. Erm, what is it?" asked Little Miss Sunbeam, struggling to hide her confusion as she unrolled it.

"It's called a Bristol Stool Chart," said Mr Dump, his face beaming. "Doctors
use it to evaluate different types of shit. My favourite is type 4 – the smooth sausage one, see? He held it close to her face so she could have a good look.

"Wow," said Little Miss Sunbeam again. "That is so thoughtful of you, I'm sure it will come in very useful."

BRISTOL STOOL

— CHART —

TYPE 1   o o o o   hard lumps

TYPE 2   lumpy sausage

TYPE 3   cracked sausage

TYPE 4   smooth sausage

TYPE 5   soft blobs

TYPE 6   fluffy pieces

TYPE 7   liquid

Mr Dump blushed.

She then, with some trepidation,
began to slowly open the other
present, fearing what she might find
rking beneath the foil paper. She
d, with some relief, a birthday
ut not just any birthday cake.

colate log! Do you get it? I
from one of my own so it's
verything!" Mr Dump's
wider.

Little Miss Sunbeam felt a little bit of sick rise into her mouth but managed to squeak out, "Thank you."

"Don't worry, it's made of chocolate!" explained Mr Dump. "I'm not a weirdo!"

"That's reassuring," replied Little Miss Sunbeam. "I'll save it till later."

If I know people like I think I do then she REALLY loves those presents, thought Mr Dump. I have smashed that out of the park.

*If you don't know what a metaphor is then go and ask an 8 year old child.

GURGLE, GURGLE, BURBLE, BURBLE.

went Mr Dump's bowels.

"Oh dear!" cried Mr Dump. "I've got a code brown emergency! The laxatives have kicked in. Can I use your toilet please, I think the world is about to fall out of my arse!"

"Yes," said Little Miss Sunbeam, "It's right at the top of the stairs. Hurry up, I've only just had my carpets shampooed!"

GURGLE, GURGLE, BURBLE, BURBLE.

Mr Dump ran up the stairs as fast as his little legs would carry him (which was not very).

He spent the next 40 minutes shitting out what would medically be described as 'rusty water'. It left him pale, clammy and visibly shaking. Little Miss Sunbeam was waiting worriedly on the landing. A long queue had formed behind her.

Back inside the temple of doom, Mr Dump came to the sinking realisation that he had exhausted the supply of toilet rolls. He had hammered his way through 8 jumbo rolls and the job still wasn't done.

He quickly evaluated his options – Option 1 was to escape out of the bathroom window but he quickly dismissed that on account of Little Miss Sunbeam living on the 14th floor.

Little Miss
Sunbeam's
bathroom

a 200 ft drop

MRANDMRSLAND TOWERS

Option 2 was to front it out but he could hear the commotion on the other side of the door and didn't really fancy that option either.

Then it struck him.

Of course, how could I be so stupid! My clothes are made entirely of toilet paper. I'm literally dressed for the occasion. So, unravelling the toilet paper from around his head and body he made the best of a bad job.

He was now though, stark bollock naked. He tried to cup himself with his tiny hands but his arms were too short so he took a deep breath and nudged the door handle open with his elbow.

"I think I should probably go home," he told Little Miss Sunbeam, who pretended to be disappointed.

"I'd give that an hour or ten if I was you..."

"and sorry about your ceiling."

Printed in Great Britain
by Amazon

34261656R00024